Love and the Rocking Chair

LEO & DIANE DILLON

Caldecott Medalists • Coretta Scott King Medalists

THE BLUE SKY PRESS

An Imprint of Scholastic Inc. • New York

E
u73-5372

THE BLUE SKY PRESS

Copyright © 2019 by Leo Dillon and Diane Dillon

Library of Congress catalog card number: 2018047310

ISBN 978-1-338-33265-0

10 9 8 7 6 5 4 3 2 1   19 20 21 22 23

Printed in Malaysia   108
First edition, October 19, 2019

Book design by Kathleen Westray

THE ART IN THIS BOOK was inspired by the paintings of Milton Avery. As Diane explains,
"He was able to convey so much attitude with only shape and flat color, without facial features
on people. That is a challenge, and we love challenges, so we decided to use flat shapes and color
for this story with only minimal indication of facial features to convey emotion. Simplifying
shapes down to the essential and achieving a smooth, flat color wasn't as easy as we expected.
Each color required several layers to achieve the desired effect." The manuscript, tight sketches
for the entire book, and four sample paintings were finished and had been put aside for other
work when Leo died in 2012. The book was forgotten and then recently discovered; Diane
completed the paintings as originally planned. The art was done with acrylic on Bristol board,
and the rocking chair is currently a napping spot for Gabby, the family's talkative Siamese cat.

For Bonnie, Lee, and Kathy

and to loving families in all their variations

IN MEMORY OF LEO AND GREG

Storytellers' Note

Every family has its own story, and no two families are the same. Yet for all of us, time passes—and as it does, our lives change. Babies are born, children grow up, parents get older, and sometimes we even lose a person we cherish. Throughout it all, love flows from one generation to the next . . . on and on and on.

Families are a great source of strength, support, and hope. The bonds that connect our family members— children, parents, grandparents, and more—often become the sustaining ties that keep us healthy and safe in a world that may sometimes seem uncertain or even frightening.

My husband, Leo, and I wrote and illustrated this book inspired by our own rocking chair, bought when we were expecting our son. It saw us through sleepless nights, lullabies, storytelling, and playtime, a beloved member of our family and witness to many wonderful memories.

The family in this story passes a cherished rocking chair from parent to child—one generation to the next. But the deeper message passed along is this: Through hard times and good times, we are here for you. We have always loved you . . . and we always will.

Mᴀɴʏ ʏᴇᴀʀs ᴀɢᴏ, a young couple stood in a sea
of chairs, searching for just the right one.

"Look at that chair over there. It's perfect for the baby's room," the young woman said.

A few days later, the rocking chair arrived in a big truck.

The couple placed it in the nursery.

Not long after the chair was delivered,

the new little person arrived.

His mother sat in the rocking chair,

singing softly to her baby.

As the little boy grew older, his father helped him
choose some favorite books.

They sat in the rocking chair, and the father read him stories while the boy looked at the pictures.

The boy loved the chair.

He rocked back and forth, pretending the chair
was a wild horse racing across the plains.

The rocking chair inched across the floor
until it could go no farther. He pulled it back
to where he started and rocked again.

Soon the boy was old enough to go to school.

He made new friends and rarely thought about the chair.

It sat in his room filled with toys
he didn't play with anymore.

Seasons passed, and the boy became a young man.

He packed his clothes and left for college.

The chair was moved to the attic. Sometimes the young man
came home to visit, but the rocker was forgotten—
unused and gathering dust.

As children grow up, their parents get older, too.
Years went by, and the father became ill.

One sad day, he passed away. The son returned home to say
a last goodbye to his father and to comfort his mother.

The next time he came, he brought someone.

"Mom, this is the woman I want to marry."

His mother hugged the woman and
welcomed her into the family.

After the wedding, the couple moved in
with the son's mother.

In time, they learned a new little person
was on the way.

The couple prepared the nursery.

And then the husband remembered the rocking chair.

"I'll go get it!" He lovingly dusted it off and
placed it back where it belonged.

Soon the new little person was born.

This time it was a girl.

The grandmother sat in the rocking chair and
sang softly to the baby. She thought of her husband
and wished he could see their granddaughter.

Seasons passed, and the little girl grew.

She sat in the chair, rocking back and forth, pretending

she was on a sailing ship, drifting across the clouds.

Soon she would be old enough to go to school, and make
new friends, and have adventures all her own. And someday,
the girl hoped, she would have her own little boy or girl . . .

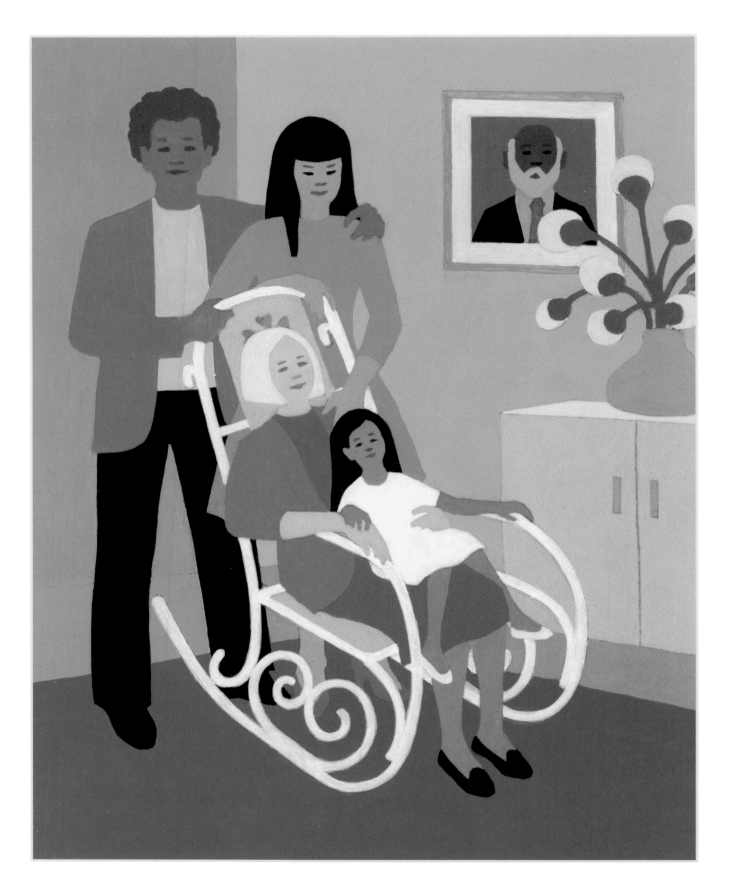

. . . and the chair would be needed again. Like her grandparents and parents before her, the little girl knew the love of her family would always be there. And that was what mattered most.